CW00865981

10 Stories to Make a Difference is a collection of ten original illustrated stories for young readers, all inspired by the theme of *difference*. The collection features a mix of well-known and emerging writers and illustrators, giving a platform to untold stories and diverse new voices. Produced by Pop Up Projects, a non-profit, UK-based national children's literature development agency, 10 Stories celebrates Pop Up's 10th birthday in 2021. Proceeds from sales supports Pop Up's work in deprived schools, marginalised communities, and with talented writers and illustrators, especially from backgrounds that are under-represented in children's publishing. 10 Stories will be an annual publishing event, with a whole new collection planned for 2022.

Find out more at **www.pop-up.org.uk**

Avital Balwit lives in Portland, Oregon. A graduate of the University of Virginia, she was the winner of *The Atlantic*'s 2020 poetry contest, and a finalist in *The New York Times* and *The Economist* essay writing contests. She writes to imagine better, brighter futures, and to delve into the mysteries of human and animal minds. Avital was one of four young winners of Pop Up's 10th Birthday Writing Competition in 2020; *That Thing* was chosen out of 100s of entries from 40 countries, and is Avital's first published children's book.

Alexis Deacon is a writer and illustrator of books including *Croc & Bird*, *Beegu*, *Jim's Lion* and the three-part graphic novel *Geis*. *Time Magazine* named his first book, *Slow Loris*, one of the 100 best children's books of all time. He's a two-times winner of *The New York Times* Best Illustrated Children's Books Award, winner of *The Observer*/Jonathan Cape/Comica Graphic Short Story Prize in 2014, and has twice been shortlisted for the CILIP Kate Greenaway Medal.

Edited by **Caroline Royds**
Art directed by **Jacqui McDonough**, Penguin Random House

Publisher **Dylan Calder**
Coordinator **Amanda Saakwa-Mante**
Designer **Txabi Jones**

Written by
AVITAL BALWIT

Illustrated by
ALEXIS DEACON

"You're telling me that thing −" Gerald poked derisively at the tank − "is the smartest creature after humans? You've got to be kidding!" The giant, vibrant-red octopus in the tank did not respond to the gesture, although Jayla felt he noticed the impolite tone. He was bigger than a labrador and looked like a wizened old man. His dark eyes blinked out of a massive bulbous forehead − but they seemed kind, as if his years had taught him not to take anything too personally, especially from snobby types like Gerald.

Jayla and Gerald were the two winners of this year's "Young Biologists of Tomorrow" internship, a prestigious research award for high school students. They got to pick a speciality (for Jayla, marine biology), decide on a summer project and visit several nearby research institutes to work on their experiments, overseen by a mentor.

Jayla was overjoyed when she won the internship. She was the best student in her junior biology class, and at the end of the term her teacher had suggested she apply. She'd expected once again to spend her holiday clearing tables at Cherry's Diner. Internships were for kids who could afford to work for free, her mum always said. But Jayla had wanted this one so badly – and it paid! It would be a dream to spend the summer doing what she loved: studying the ocean and its inhabitants.

When she found out she'd won, she immediately texted her mum, who left work early telling Mrs Ashburn – who she cooked and cleaned for – that she had an emergency. In all her life, Jayla had never known her mum to miss an hour of work, but she came straight home. The two of them celebrated by packing a picnic and walking to a nearby park. They ate and laughed and talked as the sun set. Suddenly, her mum turned to her and said, "Jayla, pitit mwen." She always switched to Creole when she got emotional. "I am so proud of you," she went on, "but know there may be people who doubt you – because you don't look like them, because your family came from elsewhere. Don't ever let it discourage you. You belong wherever you want to be."

Jayla didn't plan on doubting herself – she already knew what her summer project would be. She wanted to research giant octopuses. She'd studied them as a freshman, and ever since then, their multicoloured skin, waving arms and flexible bodies had fascinated her. She knew they were smarter than most people realised, and they had a personality and a sense of humour. Jayla wanted to learn exactly how conscious they were, and to show off their wonders to others.

It was the third week of Jayla's internship, and the first trip to an aquarium. They'd already done day-long visits to other biological research institutes to observe mice – the focus of Gerald's project – and now it was her turn. They had taken the train for an hour to spend two days at Emery Ridge, and the internship coordinator had gotten them rooms at a hotel so they didn't have to make the journey twice. Jayla felt so grown up getting her room key.

Gerald was less enthused about this trip. Initially, Jayla had been excited to meet the other winner, but Gerald was a year older than her, a senior from Brandenburg Academy, a prep school with manicured lawns and an ornate iron fence that she'd only glimpsed from her bus route. When they met, he informed her that he'd done *many* internships before, and this one wasn't even particularly special. As he took competitive strides on their brief tour of Emery Ridge's aquarium, she couldn't help notice a faint similarity between him and the blobfish – both flushed, hulking, and a little disappointed in their surroundings. Gerald was studying mice and memory. He planned to train mice to navigate mazes by giving them treats, but from what Jayla had seen so far, he didn't seem too interested in what was going on in their minds *(did they like the maze or hate it? How much did they remember from the last time through? Did they think about each other or Gerald? And if so, what?)*. His unphilosophical attitude – his general non-curiosity – baffled her.

The octopus was the last stop on their tour. They had seen eels, dolphins, archerfish, and more, and Jayla had admired the many researchers in labcoats and wetsuits bustling through the halls.

"Alright, well now you've met Frazier, it's time you see him *do* something."

The bright voice of Annie, their supervisor and guide at Emery Ridge, broke the otherwise cloudy silence. Annie, who was young and blonde, had introduced them to Frazier, the giant octopus, saying cheerily, "He takes a while to warm up to new people but he's bright as they come." When Jayla first met Annie in the lobby in her pink pleated skirt, she'd assumed she was one of the scientist's wives, and was embarrassed when it became clear Annie was a senior marine biologist who just liked wearing stylish clothes when she wasn't in a wetsuit.

Annie proceeded to show them all of Frazier's tricks. Jayla watched in awed silence as he used his dexterous arms to unscrew the lids on jars, navigate a maze, and play with some octopus version of a Rubik's cube in exchange for a reward of clams.

Gerald was unimpressed. "Mice can do that stuff, and you don't hear me making any grandiose claims about their minds."

"I bet a mouse's mind is more interesting than you think," Jayla replied.

With that, Gerald asked Annie if he could go get coffee – since this trip had nothing to do with his project. He didn't bother to ask if Jayla wanted anything. "Some distance," might have been her response if he had.

After a few more tricks, Frazier suddenly reached all of his tentacles upwards, forming a kind of crown-shape around his head.

"What's he doing?" Jayla asked.

Annie laughed. "He's begging for food. Don't you see the bowl he's made? It's like little kids, when they lift their open hands up to you, wanting something."

Jayla gazed at the bowl-holding octopus in wonder while Annie went to get Frazier more clams.

Gerald came back about an hour later and lurked behind them in sullen silence, glancing over Jayla's shoulder occasionally to see what she was writing.

It was nearing 5pm. Other researchers had started packing up. Annie asked if they were ready to head back to the hotel. Jayla was anything but ready. "Is there any way we can get in the tank with Frazier? I'd love to have a slightly closer look at him. We brought wetsuits and everything!"

"Yes, absolutely. I can set you up now in our observation tank."

Jayla grabbed her backpack and went to the bathroom to change. When she came back, Annie led them to a different room which had a trapdoor in the centre of its floor. "This leads into the observation tank," she said as she pulled it open. Through the trapdoor was a long ladder descending into shallow, clear water.

"You can wait out here if you like," Jayla told Gerald.

"What? You think I mind some water? I'll come down." He went off to change.

Jayla climbed down the ladder into the water, which came to her shoulders. She felt like a fairy-tale creature in her wetsuit, constricted but protected in neoprene armour.

The water was Jayla's element, and memories bubbled to the surface of her mind. She remembered her first time in the ocean – visiting her grandmother in Haiti. It was July, and the rain had finally stopped over the sprawling city of Port-au-

Prince. They found a semi-deserted stretch of beach near one of the many luxury hotels. The day was hot and humid, and she remembered the blinding white of the soft sand, and the relative coolness of the water. Her grandmother sat down on a rock under a palm and peacefully watched the waves. Jayla waded in as far as she could, then stood still and looked. Over the next hour she saw tiny striped fishes, an undulating squid, hermit crabs scuttling along the shore, and grey, arching shapes that she thought were dolphins further out to sea. There was so much life in that blue water, just begging to be understood and appreciated.

With those first steps into the bay of Port-au-Prince, Jayla realised that she'd found her place. She had made it through classrooms where teachers seemed constantly surprised at her knowledge and the institute where a researcher mistook her for one of the cleaning staff, and she had done it for this. Here in the water with the other animals, was the magic. Here she would become an expert, and would command the respect she deserved.

Gerald clambered down after her and plunked into the tank with a splash.

A few plastic toys floated in the water, and several artificial rocks poked above the surface for researchers to perch on. Annie lowered Frazier into the tank, a process which involved a large bucket and an elaborate system of strings and pulleys. Frazier looked indignant, his eight tentacle tips waving above the bucket's rim.

As he landed in the water, Annie's phone rang. Leaning halfway into the trapdoor, she looked worried as she listened to what the other person was saying. Then she called down, "Gerald, Jayla, my little brother just sprained his ankle at football practice. It's only a few minutes drive from here, so my mum's asked me to get him. I have to go now, I'm so sorry. I'll find another researcher to supervise you, okay? Have a good night and I'll see you tomorrow!" and she disappeared.

A few minutes later, a man peered down through the trapdoor. He had big glasses, wild-looking hair, and a distracted expression.

"Hey guys, my name is James. I research eels down the hall. Annie didn't tell me much – she seemed in a rush. What did she want me to do? Should I wait here with you?"

"No," said Gerald quickly. "Annie said we're good to stay here on our own. We're..." he hesitated, "visiting researchers. Annie just wanted you to know we're down here."

James seemed confused, but his eels must have been calling. "Alright, well I'll leave you to it. I have a bit more to do then I'm going home. The building's doors lock on their own, so just head out when you're done. You can leave Frazier here – just shut the trapdoor when you go to keep him in. I'll leave it propped open now, and don't pull it shut while you're inside. Don't want you getting stuck. My first year, one of the researchers did that while studying some sea turtles. He said it was a pretty uncomfortable night!"

Then James hurried off.

Jayla rounded on Gerald, "What on earth were you talking about?" She said furiously, "Annie didn't say any of that. We're interns, not researchers!"

"I'm sick of being babied. I've done a bunch of independent research. We can figure it out."

"Whatever," Jayla grumbled. "If we get in trouble, I'm saying it was your idea." She turned back to the octopus.

Frazier, who had slipped out of his bucket in favour of the cool water, was floating aimlessly, his eight arms like rust-coloured pieces of kelp undulating around him. His skin was turning greyer now to match the colour of the tank floor. He seemed aware of the two students, but not particularly interested in them. He floated lower in the water and moved behind one of the tank's small islands.

Jayla followed, moving slowly, half-swimming half-walking. She stopped several feet away from him, and in the same way she would greet a cat – the only animals she regularly met – squatted low and extended her hand, giving Frazier time to consider her and respond. He paused, then inched one tentacle in her direction. Realizing it wasn't long enough, he moved his whole body. His tentacle made contact, and then he sent further tentacles, one after another. They weren't violent, or even playful. They were curious – it felt like he was seeing her, and in a way he was. She thought about the octopus brain, distributed throughout its body, not just in its head like ours. This meant that, in a beautifully odd way, it could almost see with its skin.

"What are you doing?" Gerald asked. He was still standing by the ladder, the water just above his waist, surveying the tank with distaste.

"I'm meeting him."

"You met him this morning."

"No, I'm *really* meeting him."

"Don't you have tests to run on him, or something? Some kind of real experiment?"

"Of course, but I'll be back here again plenty of times this summer. I want to try to earn his trust first. It's only polite."

Gerald looked taken aback. "I guess."

Jayla and Frazier drifted around the tank together for a while. Frazier's movements were slow and relaxed – it was as if they were strolling in a park on an autumn afternoon. Annie had given Jayla a bag of clams, and she tossed one to Frazier when they came to a stop.

"You can't just feed him for nothing. He has to earn it!" Gerald said sharply.

"He *has*! Think of all the tricks he did. He's probably sick of us."

Suddenly, far above, the trapdoor slipped shut with a formidable bang. When the echoes stopped, a deep silence filled the pool. Even Frazier seemed to stand still. The only sound was the soft lapping of water against the tank's edges. Gerald quickly climbed up the ladder. He tried to lift the door, straining against the rubber seal. It didn't budge. He knocked on it as loudly as he could, but no reply came from outside.

"Do you think we're stuck in here?" His voice, often so sharp, was worried now. His brash confidence had gone. Staying in the tank meant perching awkwardly on the rocks or ladder until someone found them in the morning. It would be cold, and they likely wouldn't sleep. The prospect didn't excite Jayla, but it didn't terrify her either. She felt calm, but there was no time to appreciate this role-reversal. Gerald started banging louder and faster – she had to do something before he scared Frazier.

"Gerald!" she called up. "Let me try."

"No, I'm fine! I'm going to get it."

"No really, Gerald. Take a break and let me try."

Gerald sighed, then clambered down. Jayla climbed the ladder and examined the door. She couldn't see any way to open it from the inside, and it seemed everyone had left. Perhaps there was a security guard somewhere, but she couldn't be sure.

Frazier examined them, without urgency. Clearly, a night in the tank – if he realised that's what he was in for – didn't distress him. His expression made Jayla smile. She wanted to say, "Alright, I know you find this funny, especially after the bucket treatment. At least you'll have company down here."

They knocked and waited, waited and knocked. Jayla was starting to feel very cold. She tried telling herself she'd be alright because of the wetsuit, but it didn't calm her. Wetsuits protected people for the length of a dive, not for eight hours in the water. She saw Gerald shiver. They knocked harder. Frazier started to move faster, as if agitated by the commotion. He circled the tank with increasing tempo.

There was a drain in the far corner, and Frazier paused as if contemplating it. In a flash of motion, he stuck his tentacles through the grate, pulled hard, and ripped it clean off. Before

Jayla or Gerald could react, he had squished his body through the opening and disappeared. Jayla splashed over, sank down, and stuck her arm as far as she could down the opening. No sign of Frazier.

She turned back to Gerald and shrugged. "I guess he got sick of us." She hoped he hadn't gotten stuck in the pipe or lost somewhere, but some part of her trusted his navigation.

"Great! Now we've lost the octopus too!" Gerald grumbled.

Jayla couldn't believe what she had just witnessed. Suddenly, she remembered a news story she'd heard about an octopus from the Sydney aquarium. It had gotten sick of visitors banging on its glass, so one day it had oozed out of its tank, through the building, and into the ocean – leaving nothing but a trail of water. She grinned as she went back to her waterproof notebook and started describing Frazier's exit.

Gerald was standing by the ladder still lamenting, "I can't believe it. The octopus got free but we're trapped down here!"

She paused her writing. "That's a great summary, Gerald. You've got to admit, Frazier just showed some smarts."

"So what? Humans rescue octopuses when they're injured. Humans try to save their habitat. What do they do? Nothing!

They're smart enough to do some tricks, to get out of some situations. But not to do anything useful like us. They're just blobby, slimy, gross creatures."

Jayla was suddenly furious. She heaved herself onto the ladder and glared down at her partner. "It's always the same! People don't give a damn about anything that doesn't look like them. And they're so cruel about anything that's different! Why do you assume you know what is and isn't special, what is and isn't worthy of respect? Why can't you appreciate Frazier for what and how he is?"

Gerald looked confused. "I... I don't know. I guess I thought that if octopuses were worth my time, they'd teach me about them in school, or that they'd make something or use language or whatever." He paused. "Are you really this upset about an octopus?"

Jayla frowned, then tugged off her swim cap and shook out her dark curls. "It's not just the octopus. This internship should have gone to someone who appreciated it, someone who was going to be friendly – or at least polite – to the researchers, the animals, to me."

Before he could answer, they both heard the faint grinding of the door above them, then saw a growing crack of light as it

swung open. They saw one tentacle silhouetted against the light, and then it disappeared. Jayla scrambled up the ladder, but by the time she reached the top all she saw was a trail of water leading back down the hall. She followed it all the way to Frazier's tank, where he sat placidly among his floating balls and clam shells. Huffing, Gerald rounded the corner.

"Did he just…" Gerald trailed off.

"I think he did," Jayla replied.

"I didn't even know that they could survive outside water."

"I mean, not forever. But a few minutes, even twenty? They can handle it."

"Do you think he meant to let us out?"

"I don't think we'll ever know… but I don't think it was an accident."

On the walk back to their hotel, Gerald was very quiet. His eyes were glued to the pavement. Just before the two parted ways to their separate rooms, he cleared his throat and said, "Jayla, I owe you an apology."

"What for?"

"I should have treated this whole thing differently. I took it for granted, and I shouldn't have. I also didn't take your interests or your project idea seriously, and I guess that meant I never took you seriously. I was wrong. That octopus is way smarter than I thought. And, well, I think you deserve this internship more than I do."

Jayla smiled at him genuinely, for the first time. "Thanks, Gerald, that means a lot. And honestly, I'm just grateful to Frazier. Without him, we'd still be freezing in the tank."

The next morning, Jayla and Gerald walked back to the concrete fortress of Emery Ridge. They wrote up their observations and started packing their things. Gerald went to get his coffee, this time asking whether Jayla wanted anything. She asked for a cappuccino. She spotted Annie in the breakout room and approached her.

"Is your brother okay?"

"He will be. It's not a bad sprain, but I'm glad I went and got him. Did you guys have a nice night, was James helpful?"

Jayla decided to only answer the first question. "We had a great night. It was so cool to see Frazier up close. It gave me so many ideas for my project." She paused. "Did you know Frazier can open the tank door?"

Annie looked around the empty room and lowered her voice, "Something keeps getting into the fish tank and eating them. It's happened four times now. I suspected Frazier, because he's gained some weight and isn't always hungry when we feed him. But it would mean he's able to get out of his own tank, into theirs, and get back. I don't want to tell the lab director, though... Frazier's tank might get fortified, and I think it's pretty interesting to see how he uses his freedom. You could call it research, even..."

Jayla smiled. She remembered her own bad estimate in the lobby. Annie was a dedicated researcher who clearly cared about her field and the animals that called the ocean home. The kind of researcher she hoped to be.

"Annie, would you supervise my summer project?"

"I'd love to! I'm glad we met, Jayla, and I can't wait for your next visit."

Just before Jayla and Gerald left, they went to Frazier's tank one last time. He was rust coloured again, floating with his tentacles drawn around him. He blinked his eyes shut slowly, looking sleepy and content, so all that was left were his white eyelids. Jayla and Gerald stared into his face for a long time, searching for some hint about what had taken place the night before. Did he care for them? Did he recognize them? But Frazier just floated with an enigmatic Mona Lisa smile. Jayla and Gerald said a warm goodbye to him, and headed out into bright afternoon sunlight.

As they sat on the train home, Gerald shook his head and smiled,

"That was *some* thing."

Jayla smiled, staring at the retreating outline of the aquarium, already imagining her return.

To Peter Godfrey-Smith, whose books showed me the wonders of octopuses (Avital)

For Gary Powell, who found the beauty that others overlooked (Alexis)

Thank You!

The 10 Stories collection has been made possible through the generosity and love poured into these stories by our old friends and new, the writers and illustrators who all gave their wisdom and magic: Philip Ardagh, Avital Balwit, Jamie Beard, Sita Brahmachari, Eleanor Cullen, Danica Da Silva Pereira, Ria Dastidar, Alexis Deacon, Laura Dockrill, Jamila Gavin, Sahar Haghgoo, Jay Hulme, Daniel Ido, Krista M. Lambert, Jane Ray, Jacinta Read, Chris Riddell, David Roberts, Marcus Sedgwick, Anjali Tiwari. And through the kindness and devotion of the brilliant publishing editors, art directors and designers who volunteered their time to transform these great stories into even greater books: Emily Ball, Liz Bankes, Andrew Biscomb, Jane Buckley, Alice Curry, Holly Fulbrook, Lilly Gottwald, Elorine Grant, Libby Hamilton, Daisy Jellicoe, Txabi Jones, Ruth Knowles, Tiffany Leeson, Jacqui McDonough, Caroline Royds, Chloé Tartinville, Holly Tonks, Clare Whitston, Sean Williams. Huge gratitude to Matt Baxter and Lydia Fisher at Baxter & Bailey for donating their time to produce the 10 Stories brand, style and formats. If it wasn't for the 643 donors to our crowdfunding campaign, these books may never have made it to print - and we especially want to thank Rachel Denwood and Simon & Schuster, Sam Arthur and Nobrow, Michelle McLeod and Baillie Gifford, the CSR team at Linklaters LLP, Tim Bevan, Wolfgang Tillmans and all our former Board members for their generous support. Behind the scenes, the team and Board at Pop Up kept this great ship afloat through these most turbulent times, and we cannot thank them enough for always being part of the story no matter how hard the story gets.

Made possible by

 Baxter & Bailey    Penguin Random House CHILDREN'S

This is a first edition. First published in Great Britain in 2021 by Pop Up Projects CIC 5 City Garden Row London N1 8DW. Text copyright © 2021 by Avital Balwit. Illustrations copyright © 2021 by Alexis Deacon. The rights of Avital Balwit and Alexis Deacon to be identified as the author and illustrator of this work have been asserted by them in accordance with the Copyrights, Designs and Patents Act, 1988. All rights reserved. Printed and bound in Poland by Ozgraf www.ozgraf.com.pl ISBN 978-1-8383-2353-0